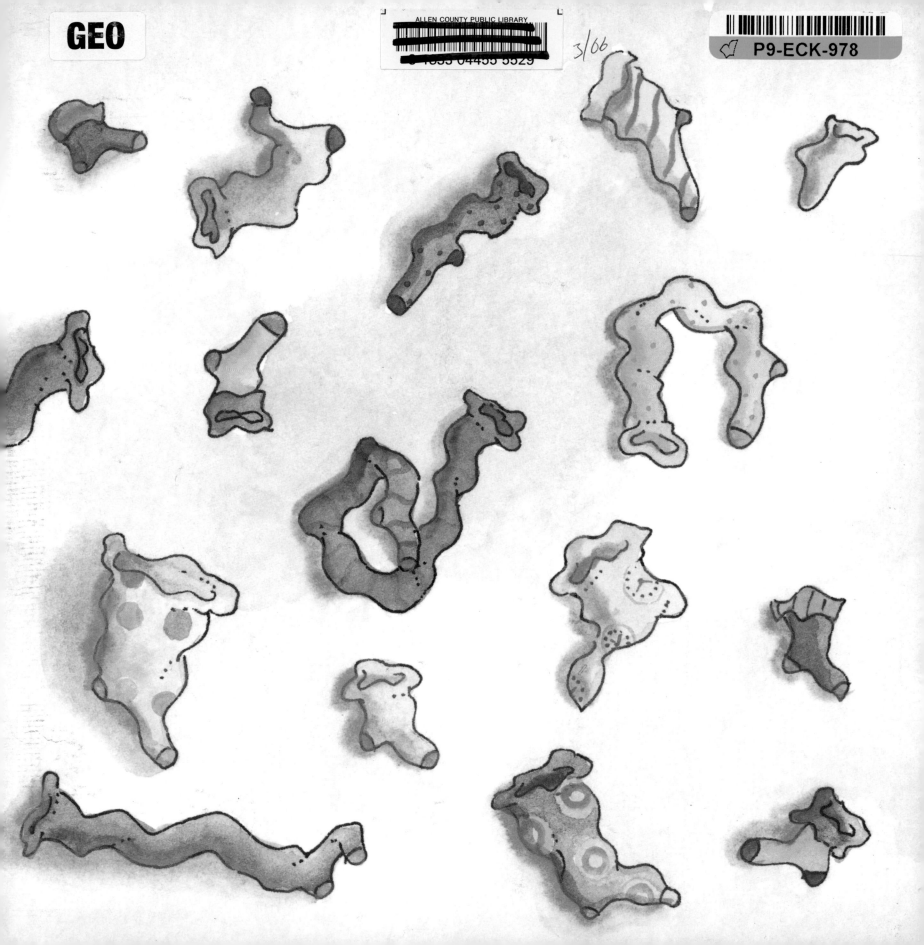

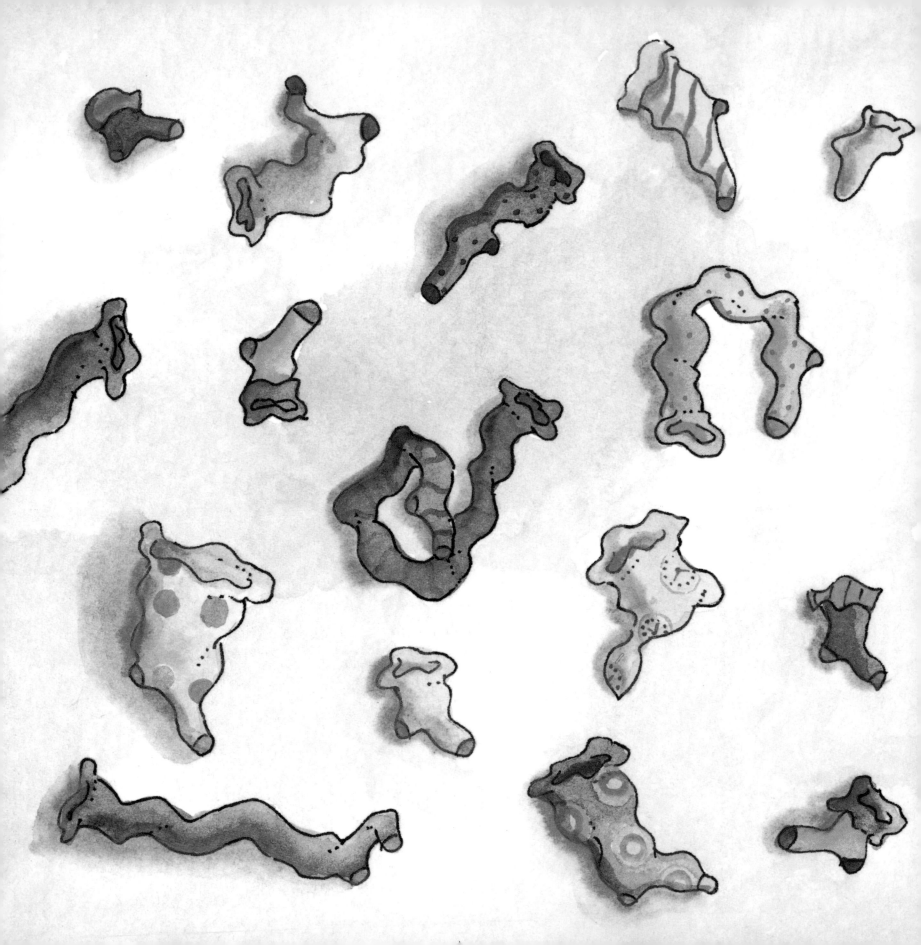

Where's My Sock?

For Jools—JD

For my mom and dad,
who have given me so much support—SR

Text copyright © 2006 by Joyce Dunbar
Illustrations copyright © 2006 by Sanja Rescek

First published in the United Kingdom in 2006 by
The Chicken House, 2 Palmer Street, Frome, Somerset BA11 1DS.
www.doublecluck.com

Library of Congress Cataloging-in-Publication Data available

ISBN 0-439-74831-3
10 9 8 7 6 5 4 3 2 1   06 07 08 09 10

Printed and bound in China
First American edition, February 2006

Display type set in Tapioca ITC.
Text type based on Chumley Medium.

Book design by Leyah Jensen

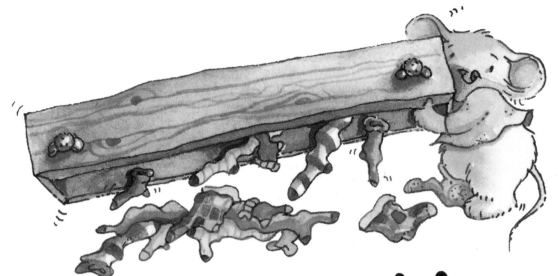

Where's My SOCK?

by Joyce Dunbar

Illustrated by Sanja Rescek

The Chicken House

SCHOLASTIC INC./NEW YORK

Pippin was mad.
Pippin was **really** mad.
Pippin was as mad as can be!

"What's the matter, Pippin?" asked Tog.
"I can't find my other **sock**," said Pippin.
"Which sock is that?" asked Tog.
"My **yellow** sock with clocks," said Pippin.
"Just like the one I am wearing."

"I'll help you find your
other sock," said Tog.

Tog looked in the sock drawer.
He found lots of socks, but he didn't
find a yellow sock with clocks.
"How about a red sock with spots?"
he asked.

"No," said Pippin.
"I want my yellow
sock with clocks."

"How about a blue sock with stripes?" said Tog.

"No," said Pippin. "I need my yellow sock with clocks."

"How about a green sock with stars?" said Tog.

"No," said Pippin. "I must have my yellow sock with clocks! I don't want to wear odd socks. I want to wear matching socks. I'll just have to keep on looking till I find it."

Pippin emptied the sock drawer . . .

. . . and the handkerchief drawer . . .

. . . and the sweater drawer . . .

. . . and the bits-and-bobs drawer.

No **yellow socks** with **clocks!**

He emptied
the laundry
basket . . .

. . . and the
ironing basket . . .

. . . and
the trash
basket . . .

. . . and the
fruit basket.

No
yellow
socks with clocks!

"Sock! Sock! Where are you?"

wailed Pippin.

"It's only a sock,"
said Tog.
"It's no use crying
over lost socks."

"I'm not crying," said
Pippin. "I'm cranky!"

"Think of the poor lost sock," said Tog. "How awful it must feel!"

"That's a thought," said Pippin.

"It must be all alone," said Tog.

"It may never, ever be found," said Pippin.

All the lonesome socks.

Socks that have lost their stretch.

Socks that have shrunk in the wash.

Socks that were never, ever worn.

"That's a lot of sad socks!" said Pippin.

"And I'm a very sad Tog," said Tog.

"I've got an idea," said Tog.
"Let's go on a serious sock hunt."

"That will be fun," said Pippin.
"Let's see how many we can find!"

They hunted socks lost under cushions . . . .

. . . and socks behind chairs.

They hunted socks stuffed into pockets . . . .

So they put them in a long line. Then they

"This is very difficult," said Pippin.
"We are making more of a muddle."

"Let's put them in a long line," said Tog.
"Then we can sort them out."

"There are still a lot
of odd socks left over,"
said Pippin,
"but no yellow socks
with clocks."

"You know what?"
said Tog. "I think your
yellow sock with
clocks is *hiding* from
us on purpose. It
will never,
ever be found."

"Then I *will* wear
odd socks after all,"
said Pippin. "I'll wear
one yellow sock with
clocks and one
plain pink sock."
And Pippin did.

"I'll wear odd socks, too," said Tog. "I wonder which pair I've got on." Pippin helped Tog take off his shoes. Tog was wearing one **purple** sock with polka dots and . . .

. . . one **yellow** sock with **clocks!**

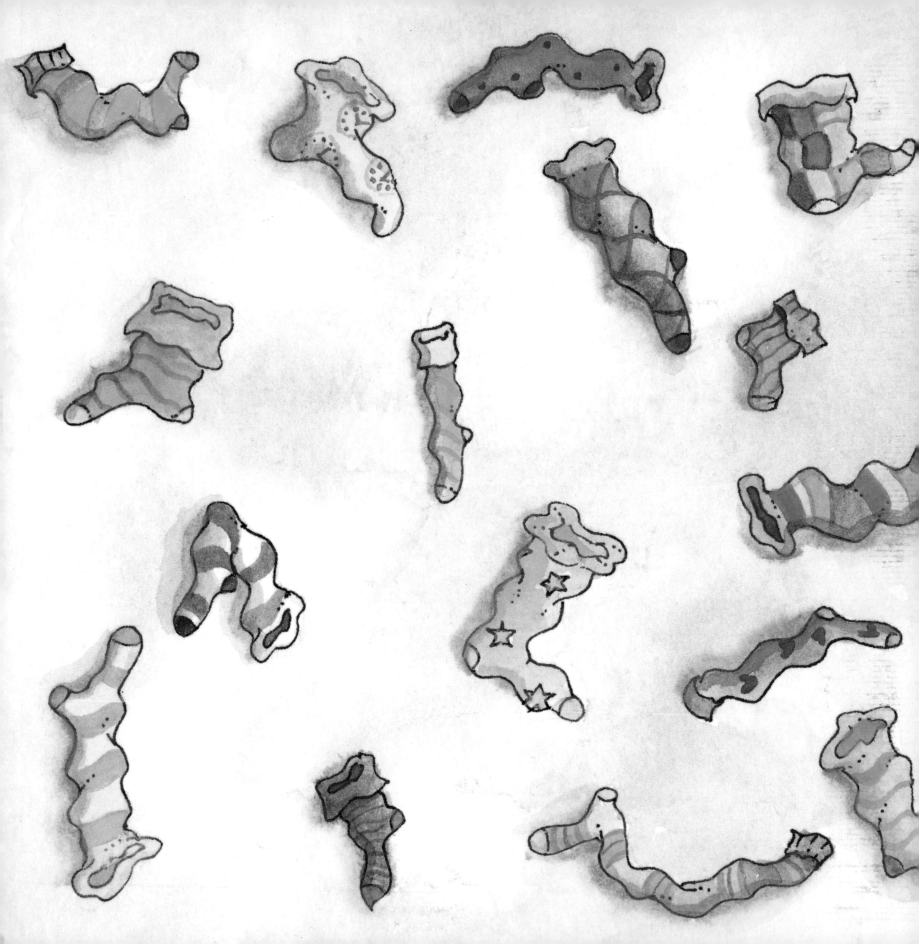